Pick me!

"Karen, you'd make a lovely Sleeping Beauty."

I narrowed my eyes. This was Karen's lucky day. But then I held my breath. All I could think of was the Lilac Fairy. I even had the lilac tutu.

"Joy," Miss Deirdre said. "How would you like to be the Lilac Fairy?"

I let out my breath. I felt ready to cry. And I almost knew what would happen next.

Miss Deirdre was looking at me, nodding. "You'd make a perfect Carabosse, Rosie," she said.

I would rather have had any other part—the mother, the father, one of the fairies. I looked down at the lilac tutu and tried to swallow the lump in my throat.

OTHER PUFFIN CHAPTERS YOU MAY ENJOY

BALLET SLIPPERS™ 3

Starring Rosie

by Patricia Reilly Giff

illustrated by Julie Durrell

PUFFIN BOOKS

Thank you to Miss Susan of Dance with Susan in

Fairfield, Connecticut

PUFFIN BOOKS
Published by the Penguin Group
Penguin Putnam Inc., 375 Hudson Street, New York, New York 10014, U.S.A.
Penguin Books Ltd, 27 Wrights Lane, London W8 5TZ, England
Penguin Books Australia Ltd, Ringwood, Victoria, Australia
Penguin Books Canada Ltd, 10 Alcorn Avenue, Toronto, Ontario, Canada M4V 3B2
Penguin Books (N.Z.) Ltd, 182-190 Wairau Road, Auckland 10, New Zealand

Penguin Books Ltd, Registered Offices: Harmondsworth, Middlesex, England

First published in the United States of America by Viking,
a division of Penguin Books USA Inc., 1997
Published in Puffin Books, 1998

3 5 7 9 10 8 6 4

THE LIBRARY OF CONGRESS HAS CATALOGED THE VIKING EDITION AS FOLLOWS:
Giff, Patricia Reilly.
Starring Rosie / by Patricia Reilly Giff;
illustrated by Julie Durrell.   p.   cm.—(Ballet slippers)
Summary: Rosie volunteers to provide the prince and the props for her
ballet class production of Sleeping Beauty.
ISBN 0-670-86967-8
[1. Ballet dancing—Fiction. 2. Sleeping Beauty (Choreographic work)—Fiction.]
I. Durrell, Julie, ill. II. Title. III. Series: Giff, Patricia Reilly. Ballet slippers.
PZ7.G3626Sr 1997 [Fic]——dc20 96-30903 CIP AC

Puffin Books ISBN 0-14-038967-9

Printed in the United States of America

RL: 2.3

For William F. Tiernan,

in loving memory

Chapter 1

"Please get off the bed, Andrew," I told my little brother. I didn't look at him.

"Please, Rosie," Andrew said. "Let me come with you."

I looked at the bed, the part Andrew wasn't sitting on.

Everything was ready for this afternoon. My best purple top with flowers, my new striped tights, and a ball of socks with lace.

Grandpa had even made lunch early: ham sandwiches with cheese melting all over the place and a dab of jelly on top.

Right now, Andrew was crying, I knew it, even though he wasn't making a sound.

I still didn't look. I hated to see Andrew cry. I knew his eyes were big, and soft, and filled with tears. I knew he was taking a tiny sniffle every two seconds.

I fished through my dresser drawer for my heart necklace . . . my special-occasions-only necklace from Grandpa.

I took a quick peek at Andrew in the mirror. Right. His eyes were filled with tears. I looked down quickly and reached for the red velvet box with the necklace.

"You'd hate the ballet, Andrew," I said. "It's too long for you."

He shook his head. "I love ballet. I love *The Sleeping Beauty.*"

I had to smile. All Andrew knew about ballet was our grandmother Genevieve's picture over my bed, our grandmother doing a *grand battement.*

All he knew about ballet was Amy Stetson next door. Amy practiced a million minutes every day.

And then there was me.

He knew I wanted to be a ballerina more than I'd want to have a skillion dollars, or be a TV star, or...

I tried to think what else. Grandpa always said everyone can be good at something. You have to love it and work at it. And I knew for me, it was dancing.

"If I can't come," Andrew said, "I might stay under the bed all week."

I had five minutes before it was time to get ready. Five minutes to practice flexes.

I sat down on the floor, legs straight, and began to work my feet back and forth. *Run away, feet. Come back, feet.*

"Rosie..."

"There are dust balls under your bed, Andrew," I said. *Run away, feet. Come back, feet.*

"I don't care," he said. "Not even if they're big as monsters, and I get buried underneath, and you'll never see me again."

I made a terrible mistake.

I looked at Andrew.

His face was streaky from crying. His legs were straight out on the bed. He was doing flexes, too. At least he was trying to.

He looked as if he was going to explode into tears any minute. "I'm at the end of my rope," he said.

"Whatever that means," I told him. I had to laugh. It was something Grandpa always said.

"All right," I said at last. "Tell Mom to get your good stuff. Get washed, get dressed."

Andrew slid off my bed. He threw his arms around my neck, almost strangling me. "Thanks, Rosie," he said. "You're good at being a sister."

"Wait a minute," I told him. "If you're going to the ballet with me, you have to . . ."

I held up my five fingers. I tried to do it the ballet way. Graceful. Dainty. Beautiful. Like my ballet teacher, Miss Deirdre.

"One, Andrew. You can't say a word during the whole thing."

"I know it," he said.

"Two. You have to pay attention."

"Yes." He nodded, looking serious.

"It's about a princess," I told him. "The bad fairy, Carabosse, puts her under a spell. She has to sleep for a hundred years, until a prince comes along..."

But Andrew wasn't listening. He was racing down the hall. "Where's my jacket, Grandpa?" he was screeching. "My robot hat? My space boots? I'm going with Rosie."

I could hear Grandpa trying to calm him down. "Don't get into a frenzy, my boy," he was saying.

While I waited, I pretended I was a sunflower with my face to the sun. I moved my

head around slowly, gracefully.

I was the Sleeping Beauty, and the prince had just kissed me.

I tried not to think about what a mistake it was to take Andrew to a two-hour ballet, when he couldn't sit still for two minutes.

Chapter 2

We rushed up the stairs and down the aisle of the Little Theatre.

"Hurry, everyone," Miss Deirdre whispered. "Rush."

I was hurrying, rushing. We were late. I held my purse in one hand. I held the back of Andrew's collar in the other.

In the balcony, two rows were empty, saved for Miss Deirdre's Dance Class, and friends.

It was so dark, it was hard to see. I stopped in the aisle and bumped into someone. A couple of kids piled up behind us.

"Ro-zzzzeeee," one of them said.

And then suddenly a light shone on a gorgeous blue velvet curtain down in front, and then on the orchestra.

Quickly I aimed for a middle seat in one of the rows and pulled Andrew in behind me. I stepped on Joy Mead's toe getting there, and nearly fell into Stephanie Witt's lap.

"Sorry," I told them both, and plunked myself down with Andrew next to me.

Andrew pointed to the man sitting in front of him. "No hair," he said. "Look how shiny—"

Good grief.

I pulled Andrew through the row again. I could hear Joy moaning over her toe. I could hear Stephanie whispering that I had dented her knees.

All around us, people were saying *sshhh*.

Finally I landed on the end seat next to the wall. I was worn out.

Now the musicians began to play. Slowly

the velvet curtain opened for *The Sleeping Beauty*.

Everyone was clapping, everyone but me. I was so excited by the sound of the music in my ears and the pink castle on stage, I could hardly move.

Hundreds of candles were lighted for the Lilac Fairy. She *arabesqued* onto the stage for the christening of the baby princess, Aurora. If I could dance the part of the Lilac Fairy, I'd never ask for anything else.

"Look," I told Andrew, as I watched her dance. "That's the good fairy. She's doing a *bourrée*. She's taking tiny steps, but see how fast she goes. Miss Deirdre calls them traveling steps."

But Andrew was pulling on my arm. "I'm hot, Rosie," he said. "Hot as a red pepper. Hot as a mustard sandwich." It was a game we played at home.

"Not here," I told him.

Someone whispered *ssh* again. Was that Stephanie Witt?

I leaned forward, but Stephanie was watching the stage. Her mouth was open, showing the space from her knocked-out tooth. She thought the Lilac Fairy was wonderful, too.

Andrew was leaning back against me now. I could feel how warm he was. I pulled off his jacket and his robot hat, while more fairies *bourréed* across the stage.

"Aren't you thirsty?" Andrew asked me.

I swallowed. I *was* thirsty.

"I need water," he said. "A lake of water. A mountain of water—"

"Andrew, you have to be quiet," I whispered into his ear. "I knew you should have stayed home."

"All right," he said. "Let's go home."

Crashing sounds came from the stage. A thunder of drums, a trumpet. Carabosse, the bad fairy, came onto the stage. No *bourrée* with tiny footsteps for her. She *jetéd*. A *grand jeté*. Arms out, she leaped from the side of the stage to the center.

As Grandpa would say, she was in a frenzy. She held out her arms to the princess in the cradle. She threw her head back as if she was laughing.

Miss Deirdre had told us all about Carabosse in ballet class. Too bad Andrew didn't know about her. His lip was out. He was ready to cry again. "It's the Wicked Witch of the West," he said. "She's going to get me."

"It's only Carabosse," I told him. "Only a story. She's angry because she wasn't invited to the christening."

But Carabosse really did look scary. She was all in black and didn't look one bit pretty like the Lilac Fairy. She looked mean and fierce as she spun around the stage.

I'd hate to be Carabosse.

"Do they have candy here?" Andrew asked.

"No, but they have a prince. He'll come along and kiss the princess like this." I leaned over and kissed Andrew's forehead.

I wondered why he was still so hot.

"A truck of jelly beans," Andrew said. "A car of Milky Ways…"

I almost forgot where I was. "A wagon of marshmallow twists," I said, trying to think of something even better.

"That's it," said a woman in back of me. "I'm calling the usher."

I stood up quickly. "Come on, Andrew," I said. We paraded back toward the aisle. From all the *ow*s and *ouch*es, I knew we stepped on the toes of every single person in the whole row.

"Where are we going?" he asked.

"To find a lake of water," I said. "And a mountain of marshmallow twists."

Chapter 3

"You look spectacular, Rosie," Karen Cooper told me on Monday. We were standing together at the barre.

"Really? Thanks." I walked one foot up my leg. Amy Stetson would say, *Hickory dickory dock. The mouse ran up the clock.*

I tried to pay attention to my feet, instead of the gorgeous tutu I was wearing. In my head I could hear Grandpa saying, "Fine feathers do not make fine birds."

I felt like a fine bird. Everyone else was wearing tights and leotards. I was wearing an absolutely perfect lilac tutu. It was net, and scratchy, but I didn't care one bit. It was loose, too, and I had to keep yanking it up. I didn't care about that either.

That's what I loved about ballet, feeling beautiful, feeling like a star. And wearing the lilac tutu made me feel better after that mess with *The Sleeping Beauty*.

I had missed seeing the rest of it. I wandered around the lobby with Andrew until he sat on the stairs, leaning against the wall, half asleep.

It wasn't until after we heard everyone clapping and Miss Deirdre came out that I knew what was the matter. Andrew was sick.

We rushed him home, and Grandpa tucked him under the covers. He looked little and skinny, and his face was red, almost as if he were sunburned.

My father brought him whistle lollipops for his sore throat. My mother bought him a new Lego set. Andrew loved Legos.

And I practiced ballet at the end of his bed so he could watch. First I was the Lilac Fairy. Then I was the Sleeping Beauty.

"Don't be Carabosse," he told me. "I'm afraid of her."

"Don't worry," I said. "I wouldn't be Carabosse in a million years."

"I'll be the prince," he said. He could hardly talk.

I *bourréed* around the bed. "You're definitely the prince," I told him.

Right now, Miss Deirdre was clapping her hands. I blinked. I had almost forgotten where I was. "Take seats, dancers," she said.

I could see she was frowning. Maybe it was because of the tutu. I was really supposed to be wearing tights and a leotard, but I hadn't been able to resist.

Amy Stetson next door had given it to me for straightening her ballet stuff ... a bunch of leotards and tutus and tiaras twisted together.

17

"Take the lilac tutu," she had said. "I haven't worn it since I was twelve."

Everyone else was rushing to the mat in the center. I *bourréed* instead, lightly, on my toes.

Over my shoulder, I took another quick peek in the mirror. I wasn't my regular self with chopped-off hair. I was the Lilac Fairy.

I looked away in time to see Stephanie Witt *bourréeing* in my path. Stephanie was the worst dancer in the class. Probably the worst in the world. At the last minute, we danced away from each other. She slid onto one end of the mat. I slid onto the other.

Miss Deirdre was waiting for us to settle down. She was absolutely gorgeous in a black leotard with a black velvet bow in her bun. I ducked my head so she wouldn't notice me, and stared down at my tutu instead.

"Wasn't *The Sleeping Beauty* wonderful?" Miss Deirdre asked now. "Didn't you love the *pirouettes*?"

Pirouettes? I hadn't seen any of that.

Everyone else was nodding, so I nodded, too. I tried to act as if I knew what was going on, even though they were talking about stuff I hadn't seen. I tried to think of something to say. I didn't want Miss Deirdre to think I wasn't listening.

Then I saw Karen waving her hand like crazy. "I have an idea," she said.

I raised my hand at the same time. I was good at ideas, too, and I had just thought of one. I waved harder than Karen. But she got to talk first . . . with my idea. "Why can't we do *The Sleeping Beauty*?" she asked.

Miss Deirdre thought for a moment. "We'd need props."

"Candles," I said. "And a castle." At least I remembered that much, and I got it in before Karen. I raced on, saying I could bring all that. I'd figure out how later.

Miss Deirdre was starting to smile. "Why

not?" she said. "Karen, you'd make a lovely Sleeping Beauty."

I narrowed my eyes. This was Karen's lucky day. But then I held my breath. All I could think of was the Lilac Fairy. I even had the lilac tutu. I knelt up so Miss Deirdre wouldn't miss it.

She did, though. "Joy," she said. "How would you like to be the Lilac Fairy?"

I let out my breath. I felt ready to cry. And I almost knew what would happen next.

Miss Deirdre was looking at me, nodding. "You'd make a perfect Carabosse, Rosie," she said.

I felt my mouth quiver a little the way Andrew's did when he was sad. I would rather have had any other part—the mother, the father, one of the fairies. I looked down at the lilac tutu and tried to swallow the lump in my throat.

A line appeared in Miss Deirdre's perfect forehead, so I made believe I was happy.

"But what about…" she was saying.

I leaned forward to hear what the *what about* was. At the same time I saw something at the window. My best friend, Tommy Murphy, was rubbing at the pane, peering in. I knew he was waiting for me.

And then I heard the *what about.*

"…a boy to play the prince?" Miss Deirdre was asking.

I looked at Murphy in the window. He was making an ape face at me. I smiled up at him and nodded.

"Really, Rosie?" Miss Deirdre said. "You can get a prince?"

I jumped. She must have thought I was nodding at her.

"That's wonderful," she said.

Everyone else was looking at me, too.

I finally had something important to say. "I guess so," I told them, looking at Murphy in the window.

Chapter 4

It was four-thirty. Lessons were over. We clapped for Miss Deirdre and Miss Serena, the piano player. We always did that. Miss Deirdre had told us it was the ballet way.

She was always telling us about the ballet way: Never wear jewelry, not even tiny earrings. You don't want them to be caught in something while you're dancing. You don't want to hurt anyone.

And another thing. No *pointe* shoes for two years. Your feet had to be strong as steel first, Miss Deirdre said. And Amy Stetson told me my feet were still like mush.

I slid out of my ballet slippers, the special pink ones from Grandpa, and toed into my sneakers, trying not to think about being Carabosse, or the mess I'd gotten myself into.

I had to hurry. Murphy would be sick of waiting in about two minutes.

I was up the studio stairs in a flash.

Miss Deirdre came to the bottom step and tapped on the banister. "Rosie," she said. "We're counting on you."

I nodded, and pushed open the heavy door.

Stephanie Witt pounded out the door behind me. She jerked her chin toward Murphy. "You going to ask *him*?" She said it almost as if *him* had capital letters.

I didn't answer.

"How about it, Rosie?" Stephanie began again. Stephanie could drive you absolutely crazy in two minutes.

I shook my head a little. "Don't say a word, Stephanie," I told her. "Not one—"

"Don't worry," she said. "You can count on me."

Murphy was outside in the alley behind Delano's Delicious Chocolates. He had piled a bunch of empty cartons halfway up the wall. He was ready to jump off the top.

Murphy was going to kill himself someday. I knew why he was jumping. He was pretending he was just hanging around, that he wasn't waiting for me. He was always there every Monday, though.

Stephanie trotted along behind me. She did that every Monday afternoon, too.

Murphy would have a fit. I didn't blame him.

Stephanie had a pile of brothers. I didn't know why she had to follow us around every two minutes.

"Ask him," Stephanie whispered. Mrs. Delano could probably hear her whispering all the way inside Delano's Delicious Chocolates.

"See you later," I told Stephanie.

She didn't move, of course. But then, by some miracle, one of the thousand Witt brothers came along. Witt number four, I think.

"You have to come home," he yelled. "Mother wants you to…"

I didn't stop to listen to what Mrs. Witt wanted. I raced along the alley to take a jump off the cartons with Murphy.

Then I looked back over my shoulder. Stephanie nodded at me, once, twice, and backed away from us. A moment later, she *bourréed* down Scranton Avenue. She had the million steps right, but the rest all wrong.

"Think of a cat chasing a bird," Miss Deirdre always told us. "One foot chasing the other. One foot right behind the other." Stephanie's feet were wide apart. She looked more like a cow than a cat.

A moment later, she disappeared around the

corner of Orient Street with Witt brother number four.

Murphy looked after her, too. He was chewing on a taffy stick from Mrs. Delano's. He pulled a piece out and stretched it with his fingers. "What?"

"What what?" I asked. I didn't look at him. I almost felt like crying again.

"Ask me what?" He pointed his chin toward the direction Stephanie had taken.

I took an enormous breath. "Listen, Murph, I know you're going to say no..."

"All right," he said, climbing back up on the boxes.

I knew that would be the end of it. He wouldn't say another word about it if I didn't ask. He dived off the cartons again, crashing the whole pile of boxes against Mrs. Delano's back wall.

She was out in two seconds. "You may enjoy

acting like hyenas," she said. "But I'd prefer it if you did it somewhere else."

Murphy and I didn't look at each other. "We're going now," I told Mrs. Delano. We shoved the boxes up against the wall. Then as we headed down the street, I tried to figure out how I would talk him into helping me build a pink castle, and worse, being the prince in *The Sleeping Beauty*.

Chapter 5

On Tuesday after school, I climbed up to the attic looking for the Christmas candles. They were up there somewhere, I knew that. What I hadn't remembered was the mess they were in: runny-looking red things, kind of bent, with green holly leaves stuck in the middle.

When I went downstairs, Grandpa was in the kitchen. He was standing at the toaster. Poor Andrew. I knew just what Grandpa was up to.

Every time one of us was sick, he'd rush to make milk toast. First came a bowl of warm milk. Next came the toast, cut up, with crusts off and butter on. They were dumped into the milk to drown. Sometimes the butter floated up to the top, and if you weren't sick before ...

I twirled around toward the table to grab a banana. I tried to remember to spot. "If you don't want to get dizzy," Miss Deirdre had said, "keep your eye on one thing when you twirl. Keep it there until you've turned past it. Then pick another thing to spot."

"Nice *chaînes*," said Grandpa, nodding at me as I twirled.

"Is that what they're called?" I asked. I stopped and sank into a chair to peel the banana. "How's Andrew?"

Grandpa shook his head. "Still sick, and mean as a snake in August."

I tiptoed into the bedroom to see. Andrew was lying on the end of the bed, one foot out of the covers, with cartoons blaring from the TV.

"Hey, Andrew," I said.

"Not nice for you to leave me alone." He looked grumpy. "There's nothing to do."

"Never mind," I told him. "I'm home now." I tried to think of how I could fix the candles. Bend them back into shape? Pick the holly berries off?

I sat on the edge of his bed and tickled his toes.

"You'd better not touch my feet," he said. "All the germs will jump right off—"

"And *arabesque* onto my toes?" I tried to smile, but I didn't feel happy. I looked out the window at Amy Stetson's house next door.

She was over there, practicing. Her head was up, her neck tall and straight. She was raising one arm up and up, then down and down.

Andrew was lying with his head over the edge of the bed. He reached out to pick up a piece of his Lego set off the floor.

"Want a cool washcloth for your forehead?" I asked. But I could see he was almost asleep again. I tiptoed out of his bedroom. "I'll be the prince," he said.

I looked back. And then he really was asleep. Too bad Andrew wasn't old enough to be the prince.

Murphy had said no.

He had given me about twenty reasons. He had soccer practice, he had to go to his grandmother's on the weekends sometimes, he had to fix his bike, clean his garage, work on his ant farm ...

Every time I opened my mouth, he threw in another reason. "Most of all," he had said, "I can't dance."

The truth was, Murphy was shy. He'd never admit that in a thousand years, but he almost never said a word in school. At home he spent most of his time checking out worms and birds' nests and stuff like that.

"What's that mess?" Grandpa was calling

from the kitchen. "What is that pile of stuff in the yard?"

I looked out the window. I could see a bunch of boards, and a pile of tools. Murphy. Good old Murphy. It was the beginning of the castle.

I made a quick stop in the kitchen. "Murphy's going to make a castle for our *Sleeping Beauty* ballet," I told Grandpa. "Not yet, not today. He's just getting everything ready."

Grandpa raised one eyebrow. "Does he know how?"

"Don't worry," I said. "We'll get it together."

Grandpa smiled at me. "Let me guess now. Is it going to be Aurora or the Lilac Fairy for you?"

I put one hand up in the air. "I don't want to talk about that now."

I went down the hall to my room. I needed to think.

That's what Grandpa always said. "Think.

There's an answer for everything. Maybe not the one you want, but still, an answer."

While I was thinking, I did turtle exercises. I stretched my head out of my shell. I looked slowly to the right, slowly to the left.

A ballerina like Amy. Like my grandmother Genevieve who had died before I was born. I stood there looking at her picture while I practiced. She wore a white tutu and feathers in her hair, and she was more beautiful than anyone I had ever seen. I bet she never had to be Carabosse.

And then I heard yelling outside. Even with the windows closed, I could hear the Witts. A person couldn't even think. I shoved up the window and poked my head out.

They were playing keep-away, I thought. They were probably running up and down the street, tearing across the lawns. All five of them, or seven, or whatever . . .

I looked up at my grandmother Genevieve.

If I stood in the right spot, it almost seemed as if she was smiling at me.

And she was smiling at me now, almost telling me...

Yes.

I had a wonderful, super, absolutely marvelous idea.

I had to turn one of the Witts into a prince.

Chapter 6

I pretended I was dancing across a stage. Stretching. Leaping. I was the Lilac Fairy. I twirled down Orient Street to see what was going on at the Witts.

Kids were chasing each other out the front door. They barreled across the lawn, down the driveway, and slammed back into the kitchen. Then they'd start all over again.

I tried to see if any of them looked as if they could dance.

Stephanie came out of the garage, carrying a

can. Yellow paint was slopping out of the side. She stopped when she saw me. A couple of Witt brothers crashed into her.

A moment later, they were all screaming. One Witt had yellow all over his sneakers; another had round yellow spots on his jeans. The driveway looked like the Lemonade Sea in the *Nutcracker* ballet.

And Stephanie looked as if she wanted to cry. I didn't blame her. Her legs were running with paint. "How am I going to finish my painting?" she yelled. "Just tell me..."

And then she remembered I was there. "Hi, Rosie," she said, as if she didn't have a mess of paint on her legs and a mess of brothers hopping over her.

"Hi," I said back, trying to act as if I hadn't noticed, either.

"What do you think about being Carabosse?" she asked, head to one side.

I raised one shoulder a half inch. I concen-

trated on Witt brother … was it number three? He was doing push-ups with his legs stretched out under the Witts' dusty van. A thin line of paint was spreading across the cement. It would reach him any minute.

"Did you come to see my bedroom?" Stephanie asked.

I blinked. You never knew what Stephanie was talking about.

She didn't wait for me to answer. She kept going, all yellow paint, around the side of the house, toward the kitchen.

I went after her. I kept one eye on the Witt brothers, trying to pick out a prince. It was hard to tell which one was which. They all had spiky hair, not as yellow as the paint, but getting there, and freckles bigger than mine. And they called each other stuff like Yo, and Skin, and Frog, and Fish.

I bit my lip. These were the worst-looking princes I could imagine.

Stephanie poked her head out the door. "Come on."

I went up the steps and into her house. It was the first time I had ever been there.

Mrs. Witt was sitting at a computer. She was tapping her foot in time to music. Loud music. We slid past her, and she nodded at us.

I tried not to look at the kitchen too closely. I had never seen anything like it. It was orange. Bright orange. One big flower was painted on the wall over the stove.

I went up the stairs behind Stephanie, keeping to one side. One of the Witt brothers was coming up after us. He took three steps at a time. "You know Frog?" Stephanie asked, pointing her free hand at her brother.

I nodded. It was the push-up Witt from a moment ago. A smear of paint covered one of his arms.

"Here it is." Stephanie pulled open the door to her bedroom.

I looked around. The room was small, with just enough room for two beds and a dresser. Everything was yellow—well, not exactly everything. Three of the walls were yellow, with spaceships, and bagels, and kids painted all over them.

"Your mother lets you . . ." I began, and closed my mouth.

Stephanie didn't pay attention. She slapped her hand against the fourth wall. It was kind of a dingy white. "See why I need the paint?" She chewed on her lip with her one front tooth.

I nodded. I was looking at one of the kids in the painting. He was jumping down the stairs.

"Is that Frog?" I asked.

Stephanie nodded. "He should be in the circus. Strong as an ox, flying around all over the—"

There was an explosion of sound downstairs. The rest of the Witt brothers raced up the stairs, down the hall, banging on the walls.

Stephanie closed her bedroom door gently. I would have slammed it.

"I practice ballet in here," Stephanie said. "At least I'm going to." She waved her arms around. "As soon as I finish painting, and fixing it up."

I nodded again, slowly. Grandpa would say, there wasn't space enough for two straws in a soda. There certainly wasn't enough room for someone to dance.

Stephanie began to chew on her lip again. Then she grinned. "Of course, I can only practice some things."

I opened my mouth and shut it again.

"You mean, 'Like what?'" she asked.

I rolled my eyes just the tiniest bit. "I guess."

"Like swan's necks, and turtle heads; like …" Her voice trailed off.

I stood there trying to think of something else she could practice.

Someone was yelling now above everyone else. "Pumpkin. Pump—"

Stephanie pointed to her mouth. "Maybe you didn't notice. I lost a tooth. I danced right into the stair post. That's why they call me—"

"Pumpkin," a Witt brother called again.

"We've got a little surprise going for my mother," she said. "It's her birthday. I painted a picture, and Skin put some wood around it for a frame."

"Pummmp-kin."

Stephanie took a last look at her room. "I need to get this finished," she said. "I've got to practice." She wiped her hands on her sweater. "I'm trying to get good at it."

Someone was banging on the garage door.

"You can come downstairs with us," she said. "See if my mother likes—"

I shook my head. "I have to go home. My little brother's sick, and . . ."

I didn't say the rest. I needed a prince, and it didn't seem as if I'd find one at the Witt house.

Chapter 7

We were lined up at the barre. I had to hold on lightly. I had a blister on one finger, from the hammer, and a splinter in another.

The castle wasn't coming along very well. In fact, it wasn't coming along at all. "I guess it'll be all right," Murphy had told me yesterday. "We'll get it going somehow."

And the candles weren't going well either. I had left them by the window to soften up. Now there was red wax all over the sill, and the candles were more runny than before.

Right now, I could see Amy Stetson in the

mirror behind the barre. She was wearing a green leotard and leg warmers.

It was strange to see her there instead of Miss Deirdre. Miss Deirdre was home with a sore throat today. She had probably caught it from Andrew.

At the piano, Miss Serena was practicing *Sleeping Beauty* music. At least that's what I thought it was. Anyway, it sounded like the music I had heard in the lobby with Andrew that day.

We were going straight ahead with plans for *The Sleeping Beauty* even though we didn't have a teacher, or a prince.

But I was the only one who knew we didn't have a prince.

When I had come in for lessons, shrugging out of my jacket, Amy had taken me aside. "Miss Deirdre wants to know ..."

I knew what she meant even before she finished.

I opened my mouth to tell her that there wasn't one prince in the whole town of Lynfield, but then I closed it again.

"Don't worry," I whispered.

"Wonderful," Amy said. "But Miss Deirdre said to tell you that he'd better start coming to classes. He has to practice."

"Yes," I said. I guess I must have looked uneasy.

"He won't have to do much," Amy said. "Just a quick little something. Miss Deirdre knows he won't be an expert."

"Right," I said, biting my lip.

And then Amy began to take us through the *Sleeping Beauty* music. "Feel the beat of it," she said. She waited while we listened to Miss Serena playing the piano.

Amy sounded almost like Miss Deirdre, I thought. Maybe because she had taken lessons for years and years.

"Who's who here?" Amy asked after we lined up.

And we told her. Three kids were fairies at the christening. Stephanie was one of them. And Karen was the Sleeping Beauty, and Joy, the Lilac Fairy . . . and of course . . .

Amy turned her head to one side. I could guess what she was thinking. "You're Carabosse?" she asked. I wondered then. Why did Miss Deirdre choose me?

I looked around at the other kids. None of them had the Albert-the-barber look I had . . . chopped-off hair the color of mud.

All of them were prettier, except Stephanie with the missing tooth. And even Stephanie—if you could put the tooth back in her mouth—wasn't that bad.

We went to the center of the room to practice for *The Sleeping Beauty*. I watched Stephanie. With her tooth or without, she was a terrible dancer. After the other day at her house, I thought she was much nicer. But she certainly wasn't a dancer.

I kept watching her. There was something… It caught just at the edge of my mind. Something about Stephanie … And I tripped over my feet and Stephanie's and crashed onto the mat.

For a moment, I couldn't get my breath. I couldn't even open my mouth.

"Are you all right?" Amy asked.

I nodded, and scrambled up.

"Now we begin," she said.

We went over and over the ballet. We used a doll for the baby princess. First the Lilac Fairy *bourréed* around the make-believe cradle. Then came the three fairies. Everyone was taking baby steps, but Stephanie was taking giant steps.

"Come on, Carabosse," Amy said next.

I *jetéd* across to the center of the room. But Amy was shaking her head. "One foot has to follow the other."

I gulped.

"Wait a minute," Amy said. "I'll teach you the way my teacher taught me." She lugged out a huge stuffed animal. "*Jeté* yourself right over this."

She grinned. "You have to leap to get over this guy, but if you fall..."

I nodded. I'd fall easily.

For the next half hour I leaped over the big stuffed thing. I tried to land with my front foot first, and the back foot right behind it.

I landed on Stuffy about forty times, and was dying of heat. I looked up at the mirror. I could see what a mess I was... hair up and as spiky as one of the Witt brothers'.

I stuck out my chin. Maybe I was a mess. Maybe I had to be Carabosse. But I knew one

thing. I was going to change the way I looked. No. Even more important. I was going to change Carabosse.

I'd ask Amy to lend me her black net tutu with the sequins. I'd wear black feathers in my hair instead of a horrible hat. I didn't know where I'd get the feathers, or some neat black earrings, but that's what I'd do.

I'd be the most glamorous Carabosse anyone had ever seen.

We practiced a few minutes more, and then the lesson was over. I went upstairs to meet Murphy, still wondering what it was that I couldn't remember about Stephanie.

Chapter 8

We were in my yard, Murphy and me. It was a great day, warm and filled with sunshine. You knew it was going to be spring any minute. And in the kitchen, Grandpa was making cocoa and chocolate chip cookies for us. You could smell them all over the place.

I looked down at the blister on my finger. I tried to look down gracefully, with a swan's neck. I'd been working on being the most elegant Carabosse anyone had ever seen.

I looked up at the sun. Too bad the day was ruined. In front of me was a horrible pink ...

". . . monstrosity," Murphy said, stepping back to squint at it. I knew he wanted to laugh. If he laughed, I'd never speak to him again.

Andrew came out to the yard in his bathrobe and woolly slippers. He had a pink sore-throat-medicine mustache. It was the exact color of the castle.

"I'm not going to be a prince in that castle," he said.

The castle was leaning to one side. I don't know how I had ever thought it would work. "You don't have to be a prince in it," I said.

"Sure I do." He reached out and touched it with one finger. "Remember? I'm going to be the prince for your ballet class."

I stood there, wondering how to tell him he wasn't going to be the prince. It was a good thing I wanted to be a ballerina more than anything in the world. All I had to do was get past Andrew and this prince business, and my being Carabosse. And I had to get

past ruining the props, the candles, and ...

That was a lot to get past. I took a breath. "I have to be Carabosse," I said.

The back door opened just then, and Grandpa came outside with the cookies, still steaming from the oven.

"Carabosse?" Grandpa said.

"Yes, but ..."

"Carabosse?" Andrew said.

Grandpa was nodding a little. "Fierce," he said. "In a frenzy."

I took a breath. I was all set to tell him I wasn't going to be scary. I was going to be beautiful.

"Strong and powerful," Grandpa said. "Genevieve loved playing that part."

"Genevieve?" I asked. "My grandmother?" I couldn't believe it.

Still nodding, Grandpa set the tray of cookies on the back step. "Give me two minutes. I have to get the cocoa."

He looked back over his shoulder. "Some people think that ballet is just about being pretty. It isn't, though," he said. "It's about strength."

"And power?" Andrew said.

"Exactly," said Grandpa.

Murphy was grinning at me. "Tough kid like you, Rosie O'Meara," he said. "You'll be a perfect Carabosse."

"That's right," Andrew said. "Carabosse is all right, I guess." But he was frowning.

"What's the matter?" I asked. I tried to push the castle up at the same time.

"Am I still going to be the prince?" he asked.

I swooped down to hug him. "You wouldn't want to be a prince for the class," I said. "It's too hard. You don't know how to dance. You don't even like to dance."

"I do so," he said.

I started to laugh. "Andrew, you're not a

dancer. You're a . . ." I stopped, trying to think.

They both said it at once: Grandpa poking his head out the kitchen window, and Murphy sitting on the grass. "A Lego boy."

"No," Andrew said. He was shaking his head hard. "I'm a prince." But he was beginning to smile, even to laugh a little, as I tickled him under his chin.

"Andrew, you're the best Lego boy I know," I told him.

And then it hit me. I knew what the matter with this whole thing was.

"Help me," I told Andrew. I *jetéd* toward the castle and gave it a shove. I could hear it cracking as it went down.

Murphy, Andrew, and I were still stamping on it when Grandpa came outside. He was carrying another plate of chocolate chip cookies and four cups of cocoa on a tray.

"A mountain of chocolate chips," I said.

"A truck of jelly beans," said Andrew.

Murphy sat up and reached for a cookie. "A spaceship of..."

A spaceship.

Murphy started to say something. "Wait," I told him. "There's something. I have to think. I have to..."

I stood up. I had just figured out so many things at once. "I'll be back in a little while," I told them. "Don't eat all the cookies."

Then I headed for Orient Street.

Chapter 9

I *jetéd*, pretending to leap over a stuffed panda.
I remembered to land first with my front foot,
and then right in back with the other. I was
Carabosse, strong and powerful.

I didn't pay one bit of attention to Mrs.
Regosa laughing a little from across the street.

I reached the Witt house in two minutes. No
one was outside. Everything was quiet for a
change.

I went around to the back and knocked on
the kitchen door.

"Get that, Frog?" someone screeched.

"I'm on top of the ladder," he answered.

I stood there waiting, until someone yelled, "Come on in, whoever you are."

I opened the back door and looked around. No one was in the kitchen. "Upstairs," someone called. It sounded like Stephanie.

I went up to the second floor slowly. I could hear music now, louder as I got to Stephanie's bedroom. No one was in there either. "In here," Mrs. Witt yelled.

I opened the next door, and stepped back.

Red. The walls were red, and the doors. And Frog up on the ladder was swiping red paint on the ceiling.

"Terrific, isn't it?" Mrs. Witt said.

They all looked at me, waiting to hear what I'd say.

"It's bright," I told them.

They all nodded.

"Wait till Stephanie does some pictures,"

Frog said from the ladder. "It's a great bedroom for me and Yo."

"I can see that," I said.

Stephanie looked up from where she was sitting in one corner of the room. "Hi, Rosie," she said. She had a paintbrush in her hand, and a dot of green paint on her nose.

"Have a seat," said Witt brother number . . . five, I think.

I looked around. The only place to sit was the floor. I found a spot and sank down.

Everyone went back to what he was doing. Frog kept painting. Mrs. Witt clicked her fingers in time to the music. Someone else was reading a book with his feet up on a dresser drawer. And Stephanie began to paint.

In a few minutes, a green tower appeared on the wall . . . and then a kid jumping off the top, a kid with spiky green hair.

"Not bad," said Frog from the ladder.

I looked up at him. "How would you like to be a prince?" I asked.

He took another swipe with the brush.

"Some prince," Witt number five said.

"What do I have to do?" Frog said.

"Be strong and powerful..." I began.

Stephanie turned around. "What a great idea," she said. "Frog could learn that stuff."

"Ballet? You're talking about that ballet thing you're doing?" Frog asked. "I don't know."

Mrs. Witt stopped clicking her fingers. "Yes," she said. "You can dance the way Stephanie can draw."

"All you'd have to do is practice," Stephanie said. "Look at the way you leap up and down the stairs..."

"And balance on ladders," said another Witt.

Frog drew a red circle on the ceiling. "Why not?" he said.

Everyone was nodding at him, smiling. And then I looked back at Stephanie. She had begun to paint a green line of grass along the bottom of the wall.

"There are a few other things," I said. "To begin with, a castle."

Chapter 10

"Don't worry," I told Andrew. "It's only me."

I was wearing my grandmother Genevieve's black headpiece. It had feathers as black as crow's wings. And Amy Stetson had lent me her black net tutu.

I stood on the front steps, doing a *grand battement*, looking as fierce as I could. And Grandpa was snapping pictures a mile a minute. "Bravo," he kept saying. "A great Carabosse."

"A late Carabosse," my mother said, "if we don't hurry."

My father herded all of us into the car. My mother, all dressed up, sat in front with him. Murphy, Andrew, sore throat gone, Grandpa, and I sat in back. We made it to Miss Deirdre's studio with about two minutes to spare.

Miss Serena smiled and gave Grandpa a special wink when she saw us. Then she went back to playing rolling music with lots of up-and-down stuff on the piano.

Everyone was there, everyone was waiting. Joy was wearing my special lilac tutu. I had given it to her at the last practice. And Karen was wearing white.

But best of all was the castle in the center of the room.

I had pictured it in pink, with pink candles, just the way it had been that day in the Little Theatre.

I should have known better. The Witt brothers had helped Murphy and me build a strong new castle . . . and Stephanie had painted it a bright shiny blue. She had painted my Christmas candles blue, too, and the whole thing looked . . . well, different . . . but absolutely super!

"Bravo, Witts," Grandpa said the minute he saw it.

And right now, Miss Deirdre, dressed in a sparkly white gown, was in the back room with all of us. She was brushing blush onto the Sleeping Beauty, and curling up the Lilac Fairy's bangs.

"Andrew," she said. "You'll be the perfect program boy." She handed him a pile of papers telling all about our ballet. "Give one to everyone."

And then she looked at me. "Ah, Rosie," she said.

I looked up at her, dying to ask for a little blush, a little curl in my chopped-off Albert-

the-barber haircut. I didn't, though. I'd been practicing being Carabosse for weeks now, strong and fierce.

Miss Deirdre put her hand under my chin. "You know," she said, "you remind me of someone..."

"Who?" I asked.

She smiled. "Me," she said.

I took a breath. I was filled with the syrup of happiness. But I didn't have time to think about it for too long. Miss Deirdre was switching on the lights in the center of the room.

It was time for *The Sleeping Beauty* to begin.

From Rosie's Notebook

Arabesque Stand on one leg with the other stretched out high in back. Arms up, one in front, one in back. Palms down.

Barre ("BAR") It's a handrail in front of a mirror. Hold on and warm up!

Bourrée ("boo-RAY") A quick small step.

Chaîné ("she-NAY") A bunch of small turning steps.

Grand battement ("GRON baht-MA") Start out in fifth position with your feet touching. The heel of your right foot is in front of your left toe. Then throw your leg up through fourth position into the air, and back down again.

Grand jeté ("GRON zheh-TAY") A leap! One leg is stretched forward, and one leg is back.

Jeté ("zheh-TAY") This is a jump from one foot to another. There are a bunch of different *jetés*. I like the *grand jeté* the best. You can also do *jetés* turning at the same time that you're jumping. I'm going to learn those soon.

Pirouette ("peer-oo-ET") This is definitely an exciting turn, or bunch of turns. The ballerina is up on one toe with her other foot pointed in back of her knee. Sometimes she turns alone. Sometimes the boy spins her, and she turns and turns and turns...

PATRICIA REILLY GIFF is the author of over fifty books for young readers, including the popular Ronald Morgan books, the *Kids of the Polk Street School* series, and many works of nonfiction. A former teacher and reading consultant, Ms. Giff lives in Weston, Connecticut.

JULIE DURRELL has illustrated over thirty books for children. She lives in Cambridge, Massachusetts.